D1276271

Donated by:

KEEP SMYRNA

BEAUTIFUL

KEEP AMERICA BEAUTIFUL AFFILIATE

Happy Reading!

The Big Green Teacher™

"Take A Deep Breath"

by

Michelle Y. Glennon

Welcome to the "My Big Green Teacher" series of books. Each book begins with an invitation from one of the six children in Mrs. Knoodle's class and is written from that student's perspective. Collect all six books and get to know all the classmates: Alfonso Bean, Sabrina Sassafras, Shabbir Jones, LeLe Lebowitz, George LaForge and Ferdie McDonagoodle.

To teachers everywhere — keep mentoring!

This book belongs to:

_____
Your Name

_____
Your Address

_____
Your City and State

_____
Your Age

For more information on My Big Green Teacher, visit www.biggreenteacher.com

Produced and published by GDG Publishing, LLC
Atlanta, GA
www.GDGPublishing.com

ISBN-13: 978-0-9797952-0-6

Library of Congress Cataloging-in-Publication Data available upon request.

FIRST EDITION: July 2009

GDG PUBLISHING, LLC
ATLANTA
2006

To all amazing kids around the world:

Please come join my big, green teacher's class. Today's lesson is "Saving Our Rainforests: Take a Deep Breath." We're going on an adventure and it's a surprise. Bring an umbrella and a safari hat.

From, Sabrina Sassafrass

Mrs. Knoodle began our class by saying:
"Class, our friends Little Bug and Pedro the Parrot, will join us today. Pedro is from the Amazon Rainforest and he will help us learn about one of our planet's rainforests. Now, close your eyes and hop on board my magic red skirt. We're going to fly to the Amazon Rainforest!"

"Hi kids!"

Rainforest Facts:

1. The canopy is the roof of the rainforest and is formed by the tops of the trees. Some trees grow 80-150 feet tall!
2. The trees of the rainforest recycle carbon dioxide into oxygen, which we breathe. The Amazon Rainforest is described as the "Lungs of our Planet."
3. More than half of the world's plants, animals and insects live in tropical rainforests.
4. 121 different types of medicines come from rainforests plants.
5. The Amazon Rainforest gets nine feet of rain every year.

"Mrs. Knoddle let me sit in front today because I'm helping teach this lesson! That makes me pretty amazing."

Sabrina

Then, the next thing we
heard was Mrs. Knoodle saying...
"Class, be sure to keep together. We're
in the thick of a hot, tropical rainforest
that is full of animals, plants and
even human life. Observe the canopy
of trees above us. I think I hear
thunder. Time to get out your umbrellas."

"Class, who can tell me how much rain the Amazon Rainforest gets each year?" asked Mrs. Knoodle.

I knew the answer even before I heard Shabbir mumble it under his breath. I said, 'The Amazon Rainforest gets nine feet of rain every year.' Then, Shabbir added, 'That's what makes all the trees grow so tall.' Then, Mrs. Knoodle added...

"The Amazon Rainforest makes up about one-third (1/3) of the rainforests on earth and makes about 15% (percent) of the world's new oxygen from it's trees."

"Listen to me, niños. The Amazon Rainforest contains muchos mosquitoes — 200 species in all. Wow!"

After the rain stopped, we started to hike again.

12

All of a sudden, the jungle ended. For miles and miles all the trees were chopped down. Our whole class became very sad, especially Pedro because his home was gone forever.

Mrs. Knoodle said, "Cutting down the rainforest is called deforestation. Because of deforestation, 20% (percent) of the Amazon Rainforest is already gone! That means a lot less oxygen to breathe."

Then, Mrs. Knoodle said, "Open your eyes!" and, like magic, we were back in our classroom. It was time to say the "Recycling Pledge."

"Class, repeat after me," said Mrs. Knoodle.

"I promise to recycle once a day. Before I throw away, I'll check to see if it can be recycled. If not, I'll find another use. It feels good to help our big home – our planet Earth. Spread the word."

Then, Mrs. Knoodle told us to get ready to sing and dance. We were going to learn another amazing song. I got out my saxophone for this one.

Jungle Rock Song

OK Everybody... repeat after me... uga, uga, uga, uga. Now take a deep breath and get ready to sing the Jungle Rock song... and 1, and 2, and 3...

The fierce and ferocious tiger waited at the forest floor,
Up at the top perched a bright and mighty bird,
Along came the rain and washed away the seeds,
And the hungry bugs at the bottom ate them right away.

(Sung to the tune of
The Itsy Bitsy Spider)

17

"Now class, this is important. When you plant a tree, it helps the air we breathe by absorbing carbon dioxide. Many rainforests are saved by planting new trees," said Mrs. Knoodle.

Then, Mrs. Knoodle showed us how to grow our own trees from seeds. The whole class grew their own saplings which are baby trees. We gave them a lot of water, a lot of sun and a lot of love everyday. Then one day, when they were big enough, we planted them around our schoolyard. We felt good knowing that our trees will help people breathe.

Thanks everyone for joining our "Saving the Rainforest" class. Remember everytime you take a deep breath to thank our amazing rainforests.

Fun Rainforest Activities and Ideas

Visit www.biggreenteacher.com for:

- More information on rainforests and conservation
- More fun activities
- Order other books or download songs or poster
- Order My Big Green Teacher program for your school

Understanding the Rainforest

THE RAINFOREST CANOPY

The very top of the rainforest is called the "canopy." Trees in the rainforest must grow rapidly to reach the sun at the canopy. Some trees grow to 150 feet tall. There is sunlight, wind, rain and variations in temperature here. Tree frogs, fruits, flowers and the animals that eat them live here.

THE RAINFOREST UNDERSTORY

The rainforest "understory" is the area between the canopy and the forest floor. It is very hot, very damp, and the air is very still during the day. Birds and butterflies live between the canopy and the forest floor.

THE RAINFOREST FOREST FLOOR

The bottom of the rainforest is called the "forest floor." Many soil-loving insects live on or near the forest floor. Seeds fall from the canopy to the forest floor where many animals eat these seeds and insects.

Rainforest Word Search

AMAZON
TREES
CANOPY
BREATHE
RAIN
OXYGEN
PLANTS
PARROTS
SAPLINGS
DEFORESTATION

```
t  r  e  e  s  o  d  l  s  s  j  a  f  w  t
k  c  c  o  r  x  l  l  a  k  b  c  r  s  i
u  c  m  p  n  y  e  y  b  i  a  a  w  p  g
b  o  r  f  s  g  b  t  r  m  x  n  g  l  p
u  n  s  c  x  e  n  i  e  s  b  o  z  w  q
r  j  r  i  w  n  d  l  a  s  a  p  i  w  s
a  a  o  b  h  e  u  c  t  a  o  y  u  t  x
i  c  p  l  a  n  t  s  h  i  e  a  r  p  n
n  o  n  f  e  g  b  h  e  m  l  n  e  l  i
o  w  s  a  p  l  i  n  g  s  x  t  i  w  z
n  c  j  b  n  e  u  e  n  a  r  s  u  s  p
i  c  m  o  e  s  d  b  r  e  a  t  h  e  r
q  o  r  f  t  g  b  k  j  r  r  l  p  e  d
s  j  d  i  w  o  d  l  p  a  r  r  o  t  s
k  s  b  a  k  p  s  a  w  i  s  d  u  s  o
u  c  y  e  t  b  a  v  a  n  o  s  r  p  a
m  d  e  f  o  r  e  s  t  a  t  i  o  n  b
```

Map of the World's Rainforests

The map below shows the location of the world's tropical rainforests. Rainforests cover only a small part of the earth's surface – about 6% (percent), yet they are home to over half the species of plants and animals in the world. More than half of the world's rainforests are located in three countries on three continents.

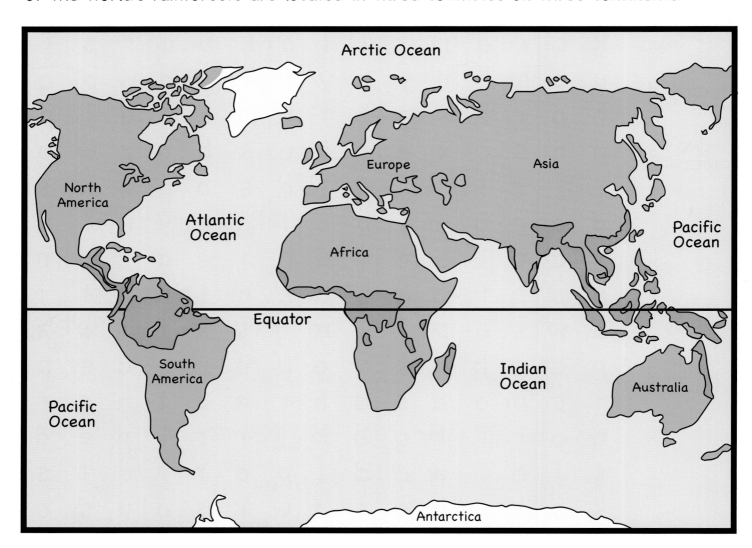

Rainforests of the world

Color Your Own Rainforests

Pick your own colors for the world map. Be sure to pick a good color for the rainforests.

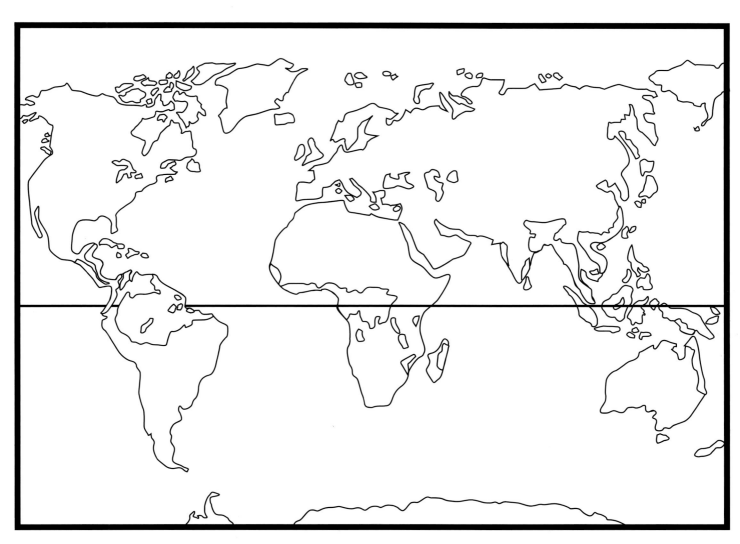

☐ Rainforests of the world

Take the "Kids for Earth" Pledge

Kids for Earth

TAKE THE PLEDGE

"I promise to recycle once-a-day. Before I throw away, I'll check to see if it can be recycled. If not, I'll find another use. It feels good to help our big home — our planet Earth. Spread the word."

Did You Know?

Facts about deforestation:

- 1.5 acres of rainforest are lost every second.
- Over 34 square acres of rainforest are burned every 23 seconds.
- Up to 78 million acres of rainforest are destroyed every year.
- 80-90% of Earth's remaining rainforest is predicted to disappear by the year 2020.
- Deforestation is the second principal source of atmospheric carbon dioxide, contributing 25% of carbon emissions to our atmosphere.

Learn more about some of the causes of deforestation:

- Logging
- Cash Crops & Cattle Ranching
- Fuelwood
- Large Dams
- Mining
- Tourism
- Overpopulation

Learn more by going online:

www.rainforesteducation.com
www.ClimateProtect.org
www.StopGlobalWarming.org
www.rainforestconservation.org
www.slwcs.org
www.EverGreen.edu
www.ourforests.org
www.worldwildlife.org
www.Conservation.org
www.wilderness.org
www.heartofthehealer.org
www.mongabay.com
www.conservationrainforesttrust.org
www.forests.org
www.funedesin.org